Safiri the Singer

Safiri the Singer

East African Tales

Eleanor B. Heady

Illustrated by Harold James

Follett Publishing Company
Chicago

ISBN 0 695-40244-7 Titan Binding
ISBN 0 695-80244-5 Trade Binding

Library of Congress Catalog Card Number: 76-161551

First printing

Contents

Author's Note

The tradition of the wandering storyteller is one that is dying out in Africa. Modern communication has made his once valuable services almost useless. Still, he may sometimes be found in remote places, going from village to village with his songs and stories. In times past, the msafiri, or safiri (safeeree), a traveling minstrel, was a vital link between the tribes of Africa. He was largely responsible for the spread of stories over wide reaches of the continent.

This book covers a mythical storytelling journey

from the forests near Lake Victoria to the seacoast on the Indian Ocean. The stories are those that are suitable for the people Safiri meets and the locations where he stops for rest.

Wandering minstrels nearly always played musical instruments, simple ones they made from things at hand. A common sounding box was a gourd, as with the gambusi (gamboosee), a kind of thumb piano. Some of these were made without sounding boxes. Minstrels often played simple two- and three-string violins.

East Africa is a varied land, rising from the lowlands of Uganda to the towering snow-clad peaks of the Kenya highlands around Kitingara or Mt. Kenya. Then the land slopes gradually to plains and rivers, grasslands and woodlands, to the steaming coast of the blue Indian Ocean. Mt. Kilimanjaro in Tanzania, towering above the surrounding plain at nineteen thousand seven hundred feet is the highest point in all Africa.

The people of this area are as varied as the landscape. The farming Kikuyu live next to the wandering Masai herdsmen. At one time there were many hunters in East Africa, but this way of life is disappearing.

Some of the stories in this collection are the popular African animal trickster tales, stories in which a weaker creature outwits a stronger opponent. Also contained in this volume are a number of *why* stories. Just as every storyteller changed his tale to suit himself or his audience, I have changed these. The words are mine, but great care was used to keep the African backgrounds authentic.

I am deeply indebted to many African friends for telling me stories. I am also grateful to the staff of the McMillan Memorial Library in Nairobi for allowing me to use their excellent collection of information on Africa. My special thanks to Mrs. Lois Karika, a Kenyan, for helping me with some of the African names. Without the help of all these people this book would have been impossible.

Pretend you are traveling with Safiri, the singer and storyteller. Listen as he spins his tales at village campfires across the wide reaches of East Africa. Hear the tinkle of his gambusi.

The Monkey Princes

Many years ago Tebetebe was monkey king of
the forest. He had three children; Tebe,
Bururu, and Nyani. Tebetebe was a wise and good
king, ruling with justice and kindness. His rule was
long.

The three sons, Bururu, Tebe, and Nyani grew
up with great freedom. They roamed the green
forest, played in its trees, and never worried about the
future. In all the forest, there were no other children
as carefree as the sons of Tebetebe.

When Tebetebe was very old, he sent for his

messenger, Sungura, the hare. "I shall die soon, Sungura. Bring my three sons so I may see them once more."

Sungura set out through the forest, looking in all the trees for the king's sons. Finally, high in the branches of a giant mvule tree, he spied Bururu. "Come, hurry, Bururu," he called. "Your father, Tebetebe, wishes to see you before he dies."

Bururu, who was having a very good time swinging in his treetop, called down with a laugh, "I don't believe you. My father has always been very strong. This is only a trick to keep me from my play. Go away, Sungura. Tell my father I'll come home later." With a laugh, he jumped to a nearby tree and was off through the forest before the startled Sungura could reply.

Shaking his head sadly, the faithful hare went on to find the other sons. At the foot of a huge palm tree, eating a fruit that had fallen to the ground, was Nyani. "Come, hurry, Nyani," called Sungura. "Your father, Tebetebe, is near death and wishes to see you."

"Really, Sungura, you spread such rumors. Everyone knows that my father has always been very strong. He can't be dying yet. However, if he really wants to see me I shall come when I have finished eating this delicious palm fruit. Go away, Hare, and stop bothering me." With that, the carefree Nyani turned his back on Sungura and continued to eat.

Sungura hopped on, looking high in the trees and all through the forest for Tebe, the remaining son. After much searching, he came upon him asleep high in a tree. "Tebe," he called softly, "Wake up, Tebe, and come with me."

The young monkey opened his eyes slowly. "Who called me?" he asked sleepily.

"It is I, Sungura, your father's messenger. Your father needs you, Tebe."

"Needs me? But why? My father has always been able to rule his kingdom without me."

"You don't understand, Tebe. Your father is very old. He is dying and wishes to see you before he goes."

"My father, dying?" exclaimed Tebe in shocked disbelief. "If that is so, I must go to him at once." He was off toward his father's tree home before Sungura had time to say another word.

When Tebe arrived at the home of his father, the old king was overjoyed. "Welcome. How glad I am you have come," he said. "Because you were the first to do my bidding, you shall be the next king. So that all shall know you are king, I give you a red tail, a white nose, and white whiskers. You shall be known as Tebe, the redtail, king of the forest."

"I shall try to rule as wisely as you have, Father," said the young prince.

"Good, my son. Now go to the forest pool and wash. When you come out of the water, you will see your new colors in the surface of the pool."

Tebe went sadly to the forest pool and did as his father commanded.

Bururu sat in his treetop for a long time after Sungura had left him. Perhaps he should go. The king was old. Maybe that hare wasn't fooling. Feeling a little guilty, Bururu jumped to the next tree, swinging and leaping through the branches toward his father's home.

When Bururu arrived at the tree home of Tebetebe, the old king was pleased to see him, saying, "Welcome. I'm glad you've come, my son. Your brother, Tebe, was here before you. He will be king because he was quick to do my bidding. You, who were second to come, shall be prime minister. Your robes of office shall be long black-and-white fur. Now, go to the pool in the forest, wash in the water, and when you come out, you will see your new colors in the surface of the pool. You shall be known as Bururu, the colobus."

"I shall try to be a good prime minister. Goodbye Tebetebe, my father," said Bururu as he sadly swung away through the trees.

Nyani, the third son, sat for a very long time eating palm fruit and thinking of what the hare had told him. Perhaps that old Sungura wasn't fooling. Perhaps his father did want him. He spit out the last of the seeds and made his way slowly through the forest to his father's home.

When Nyani arrived at the royal tree in the forest, his father was very weak. Tebetebe's old eyes looked at the young monkey scornfully. "Why did you take so long to come?"

"I was eating palm fruit."

"Eating palm fruit! Was your stomach more important than the wishes of your dying father? Because you are a thoughtlesss son, you shall be the lowest in the monkey kingdom. You shall be known as Nyani, the baboon, and be hated by all the forest people. Your nose will grow long and your fur will be a plain gray color. Now let me die in peace," said Tebetebe.

To this very day, the children of Tebetebe live in the forest. Tebe, the redtail, is king. Bururu, the colobus, is prime minister. But Nyani, the baboon, is the lowest subject in the monkey kingdom.

The Crocodile's Cousin

In a pool in the river lived Mamba, the crocodile. On the bank near his pool, he had a garden in which he grew *wembe,* a kind of grain. One fine bright day he dug up his garden with his short front feet and carefully planted his seeds, then slithered back into the water to wait for his crop to grow.

In the woods nearby lived a family of chickens, who came each day to the crocodile's pool to drink. One day Kuku, the cock, came leading his flock past the newly-dug garden. He saw the freshly turned earth and called his family to look for worms there. They found the wonderful millet seeds. They ate them all, scratching merrily to find every one. Then they went to the pool to drink.

Mamba rose from the water, shouting, "Thieves! You have ruined my garden!"

The chickens ran back from the river, all but Kuku, who stood still and crowed loudly, saying, "Mamba, the crocodile, is my cousin."

"What do you mean, Kuku, saying I am your cousin?" shouted the crocodile.

The cock answered, "But of course you are our cousin. Relatives always share their food. You know that as well as I."

This made Mamba very angry, and he screeched, "Come closer and I'll make you share with me!"

"I will come back and talk to you tomorrow," said Kuku. Then he ran after his family into the bush.

Kuku, the cock, and his family returned next morning to drink at the crocodile's pool. They brought with them, Kanga, the guinea fowl, and many other birds.

When Mamba saw them coming, he peered from the water and asked, "Kanga, and all you other birds who drink here, please tell me why it is that the chickens say that I am their cousin."

The birds were silent. They looked puzzled.

"Tell me, Kanga, do I have feathers like you?" asked the crocodile.

"I see none," answered the guinea fowl.

"Do I fly through the air like a bird?"

"I've never seen you fly," replied Kanga.

Then Kuku spoke, "I still say Mamba is our cousin."

"But why do you say that?" asked the guinea fowl.

"Because Mamba was first an egg, then came out and became a crocodile. We were also first eggs, then became fowls and birds. Since all of us came from eggs, then we must be related."

"How ridiculous!" hissed Mamba. "I suppose next you'll say I scratch for insects, too."

"Well, you could. You planted millet," said Kuku.

"Yes, and you stole it—you and your thieving family," shouted Mamba. "You are only trying to make me believe you are my cousin so that I won't punish you for your rascality."

"Oh, no, great king of the pool. That is only because we respect you so much," insisted Kuku.

Then Mamba said to all the birds, "Tell me, you

who have two legs, do I who have four look so much like you?"

"No, no!" shouted all the birds.

"Do you think I am your cousin?"

But the birds were silent. They didn't want to offend Kuku, who was really their cousin.

Then Mamba rose to his full height at the edge of the water and said in a very loud voice, "I am angry with Kuku and his family for stealing my seeds and then pretending to be my cousins. From this day on they may not drink from my pool in the river."

"And what about the birds and the guinea fowls?" asked Kanga.

"You may drink at the pool, as you have done nothing to harm me, but the chickens will never be allowed here again. If they dare to come, I shall eat them all."

Then Kuku and his family went away to the village. From that day, they lived with the people and drank from pots of water set out for them.

But Kanga, the guinea fowl, and all the other birds remained in the bush and drank from the pool in the river.

Visitor

Once long ago Sungura, the hare, and Kamba, the tortoise, were friends. They attended all the same parties and were called the fast one and the slow one.

One day Kamba, the tortoise, stopped at the home of his friend and shouted, "Hello, Sungura, may I come in?"

"Welcome," said the hare as the tortoise crept slowly through the doorway. "What brings you my way so early?"

"It is this, friend. I have been invited to dine

with my cousins on the other side of the wood. They asked that I bring you, too. How about it? Can you come with me?"

"I certainly can," said Sungura. "An invitation to dinner is something I never refuse."

"Very well, Sungura. I'll stop for you around noon. It's a rather long journey." And Kamba backed slowly out the door.

"Long journey, indeed!" muttered Sungura as soon as his friend had gone. "I could get there in thirty-six leaps, seven hops, and a jump."

When Kamba stopped for Sungura, he found the hare anxious to start. As the tortoise plodded slowly along, his friend hopped about or sat still, waiting. And all the while he talked. "Kamba, did you know that I have a second name?"

"No. What is it?"

"My second name is Visitor."

"Visitor? How queer!"

"Not queer at all. I'll bet your cousin, Ngu, knows my name."

"Sungura Visitor. I still say it's a queer name, but if you say that's your name, guess that's it." And the tortoise crept on.

Now, when the two friends arrived at the home of Ngu, the tortoise's cousin, they found that generous gentleman waiting anxiously. After a friendly greeting, he took them into his house, where bowls were set for two. Guests in all properly conducted households are left to eat alone.

Slapping his hands together, Ngu called to his wife, "Come my dear, our visitors have arrived."

"See," whispered Sungura to Kamba. "He knows my name."

"Yes, he did say 'visitor,' " agreed the tortoise.

Ngu called again, "Bring food for our visitors."

"See, they are bringing me food," said Sungura.

"But isn't some of it for me?" asked Kamba.

"Oh, yours will come later. I'll eat mine as they bring it."

So when a large bowl of steaming porridge was set upon the table, Sungura helped himself generously. Kamba waited for his bowl to be brought. Next, the wife of Ngu came with a large bowl of mushrooms, saying, "The freshest mushrooms in the woods for our visitors." Sungura ate these, too. When finally a large pot of plums was placed in front of the two, Kamba left the table saying, "Don't eat until I return. I want to ask some questions."

Now, as soon as Kamba was gone, the crafty Sungura put the plums into his knapsack.

Kamba returned with Ngu, saying "My cousin says the food was for both of us. You have eaten it all, even the plums, and I am hungry."

Sungura pretended surprise. "I am sorry. You said the food was for Visitor, and that is my name."

"That was never a name for anyone," declared Ngu. "You are a most ungracious visitor, and I shall not ask Kamba to bring you again."

Sungura sat with his head in his hands pretending to be sorry. While he was sitting, Kamba noticed the bulging knapsack and peeked inside. Sure enough—plums! He whispered something to Ngu and crept into the sack with the fruit.

When the hare raised his head and looked around for the tortoise, he saw only cousin Ngu. "Where is Kamba?" he asked.

"He went home to eat. He is very hungry, and we have no more food here."

"Then I shall be going, too," said Sungura. "Thank you for the feast." Taking up his knapsack, the hare began the journey home. But the knapsack seemed heavy, very heavy. Soon he sat down on a rock beside the path. "Maybe if I eat some of the plums it won't seem so heavy," He opened the sack.

Kamba, the tortoise, looked up at him. "Hello, Sungura. Surprised?"

"I thought those plums were heavy. Where are they?"

"Right here," said the tortoise and rubbed his stomach and grinned. "They were delicious."

"Guess you win this time," said Sungura. "You may be slow when it comes to walking, but there's nothing slow about your thinking."

The Coucal's Voice

Once an elephant lived in the forest. Nearby in the trees lived Koku, the coucal. The two were great friends, talking together daily. One morning they decided to go on a journey to the edge of the forest. Tembo, the elephant, crashed through the bush, while overhead, Koku flitted and sang from the treetops.

When they reached the place where the forest ends in tall grass, Tembo raised his huge head, waved his long trunk toward the treetops and called, "Friend Koku up there, aren't you hungry?"

"Indeed, I am," replied the coucal.

"We're a long way from home," said the elephant. "Wish I could send a message to my wife. If I could make her hear me, I'd tell her to prepare a good dinner and have it ready when we return."

"A fine idea, Tembo. I should like to send the same message to my wife."

"My voice is great," said Tembo. "Perhaps I can call loudly enough to make her hear me."

"I shall try the same thing," said Koku. "I am famous for my voice."

"You? Why your voice, although very pleasant, is not strong enough to be heard halfway through the forest," laughed the elephant.

"You might be surprised at my voice," said the coucal. "How about a contest, Tembo? We'll both call to our wives to prepare dinner. I'm sure my wife will get my message before your wife gets yours."

"Ho, ho! What a joke," roared Tembo.

"I'm serious, friend," insisted Koku. "You call first."

Then Tembo raised his trunk high, opened his huge mouth and trumpeted shrilly, "Whee-eee-eee, prepare dinner for mee-eee-ee!"

"That was a big noise, Tembo. Now I shall try." Koku sat on the highest treetop and called softly, "Cuckoo, cuckoo, cuckoo-oo-oo. Fix food, fix food, fix food."

"Do you really think your wife will hear that?" asked the elephant.

"I think she will. Let us start home now."

Back through the woods went Tembo. Through the treetops above him flitted Koku. They came first to the home of the elephant.

"Here we are, wife," called Tembo. Is dinner ready?"

"Dinner? And why would I have it ready when I didn't know you were coming?" asked his wife.

"Didn't you hear me call from the edge of the forest?"

"No, of course not. That is too far to hear even your loud voice, Tembo."

Then Koku spoke. "Let us go to my house, friends. I'm sure my wife heard me and will be ready with a fine dinner."

"Ridiculous," sniffed Tembo. "We'll go just to see how wrong you are."

When Koku and the elephants arrived, they were

greeted by the coucal's wife. "Welcome, my husband and friends. Dinner is ready."

"Dinner ready? How did you know we were coming?" marveled Tembo.

"My husband sent me a message," replied the coucal's wife.

"I can't understand how such a tiny bird with a soft voice could make himself heard across the forest when I with my loud trumpeting was not heard," puzzled the elephant.

"Don't you know the coucal's secret, Tembo?" asked Koku. "We always pass a message along. Mine was repeated by my cousins from the treetops all across the forest and so came to my wife. By working together, we made one small voice go a long, long way."

The Strong Chameleon

Tembo, the elephant, was king of the forest. But strong as he was, he feared man and Kebu, the tiny chameleon. His fear of man was easy to understand. Man hunted Tembo for his long ivory tusks.

Kebu was jealous of the great power of Tembo and his influence with the other animals. He planned a way to humble the elephant. Meeting him in the path one day he called out, "Oh, great Tembo, all the animals say you are the strongest in the forest. But

I, Kebu, should like to have you prove it. I believe I am stronger."

Tembo, from his great height, looked for the chameleon. But Kebu changed from the brown of a tree trunk to the bright green of the grass beneath his feet.

The elephant shouted, "Oh, trickster! You changer of color! Of course you are stronger in your ability to make yourself invisible. When it comes to real strength, you could never perform a mighty feat like pulling down a tree trunk or stamping a hole into the ground."

"Ha, ha and ho, ho," laughed the chameleon. "I shall challenge you to a contest. We shall see who is stronger."

"Fair enough, Kebu. But I warn you, you shall be defeated," rumbled Tembo.

"Tomorrow morning, after we have slept, let us meet here in this path and see which of us can stamp the deepest hole into the ground. If yours is larger, I shall never again doubt that you are the strongest animal in the forest, oh huge and noble Tembo." Then Kebu made himself visible right in front of the elephant's trunk.

"Agreed. I shall be here at sunrise tomorrow.

Good day, Kebu." With a grunt, Tembo rumbled off down the path.

Now Kebu set to work in earnest in order to defeat Tembo in the coming contest. First he dug a deep hole in the path, then covered it with a very thin layer of sticks. Next he added long grass and leaves so that it looked exactly like the rest of the track. He climbed to his bed in the tree and waited for morning.

Early, just as Jua, the sun, was rising, Tembo came lumbering down the path.

The chameleon, who was watching, called out, "Wait for me."

Tembo stopped and waited until he saw Kebu at eye level, then said with a sneer, "Since you are so small and I so great, you try first. You will be discouraged after I make my hole in the ground."

"Very well," answered the chameleon.

The two walked on a few steps and Kebu said, "Shall we try here?"

"Looks as good as any place to me," agreed the elephant.

Then Kebu, the chameleon, gave one great leap into the air and came down with a plunk right where he had dug his hole the night before. Down he sank into the earth.

Tembo peered with his nearsighted eyes. He was very puzzled. Right then he decided that he could never stamp such a hole into the earth. He was so frightened by the magic of tiny Kebu that he ran down the forest track as fast as he could go.

To this very day all children and grandchildren and great-grandchildren of Tembo, the elephant, are afraid of chameleons because they believe them to be very strong.

The Doctor's Servant

Once very long ago there was a frog called Chura, a doctor of great renown. Chura knew how to make a wonderful ointment. He kept this ointment in a large handsome calabash with a very long narrow neck. He dipped it out with a long-handled spoon when he needed it for his patients.

After all the ointment was gone, Chura tried very hard to clean the calabash. But the neck of the vessel was so narrow that he couldn't get his hand inside.

While the frog was considering ways to clean his

beautiful calabash, Panya, the mouse, came by looking for work. "Good day, Doctor Chura," he said. "I am very much in need of a job so that I can earn a few kernels of grain. Nearly everything in the bush has been eaten. Can you help me, for I am hungry?"

"Perhaps we can help each other," said Chura. I have here a very fine calabash that contained ointment. I should like to use it again, but before I can do that it must be cleaned. If you can figure out some way to clean it, I will reward you well."

"How generous of you, my friend," Panya, the mouse, started thinking. First he tried to get into the calabash, but the opening was too small to admit his slender body. Then he ran around and around, looking for a hole into the side of the vessel. Finally he stopped and said to the frog. "I can clean your calabash for you, but I will first have to gnaw a door into the side with my sharp teeth."

"How stupid! Can't you see that such a hole would ruin the calabash? It would no longer hold my ointment. If you have no better proposal than that then go find work somewhere else." The disgusted Chura went into his house and Panya went sadly down the path.

Then along came Bui, the spider. He stopped in front of the doctor's house and called, *"Jambo* to you, Chura."

The frog put his head out. "Hello, Bui."

"I am looking for some place to spin my web. May I spin it in this calabash beside your door?"

"No, Bui, you may not spin in my calabash. I want to find some way to clean it so that I may use it again for ointment."

"I didn't think you wanted it since it was outside your door. I must find some other dark place in which to make my web. *Kwa heri,* Doctor." And Bui sped off down the path.

From the direction of the village came Dudu, the cockroach. He, too, was looking for work. *"Jambo,* Doctor Chura," he said. "I am looking for work. Is there any job I can do for you in exchange for a few crumbs?"

"Yes, perhaps you can help, Dudu. See this calabash. It is a very fine one, and I should like to use it again to hold some more of my wonderful ointment. Because the neck is so narrow, I cannot get my hand inside to clean it. Perhaps you can find a way to clean it for me."

"Good. I shall try," agreed Dudu.

"Very well. I must go to the village to buy supplies to make my ointment. When I return, I hope to find the calabash clean." Chura hopped off down the path.

When the doctor had bought his supplies, he returned to his hut to find the cockroach sitting proudly on the side of the calabash. "I have done as you asked," he said. "Hold the calabash up to the light and look inside."

Chura lifted the calabash and found it shining clean. "How did you do it?" he asked.

"Just crawled inside and ate away all the dirt," answered Dudu.

"How would you like to stay with me in my house and do all my cleaning?" asked the frog.

"A-i-i-i, I should like it very much," replied the cockroach. "Nothing is more fun than cleaning up the crumbs."

To this very day, cockroaches clean their masters' houses.

Dirty Hands

"**P**lums! Lovely ripe plums!" exclaimed Kamba, the tortoise, as he gazed up into the tree. There they hung, red and ripe. But Kamba couldn't climb.

"How I wish I could get some of those plums." Sadly the tortoise crawled away, marveling at the good fortune of those who could climb trees. He was so deep in self pity that he didn't see Nyani, the baboon, approaching.

"*Jambo,* Kamba," called Nyani. "Why so glum?"

"Oh, what a start you gave me, Nyani. I'm only wishing I could climb trees!"

"Climb trees? You—climb trees? That's a good one! Why, if I had a shell like yours for protection, I'd never worry about climbing trees. You should be glad you don't have to bother with climbing," laughed the baboon.

"But, you don't understand, Nyani. I only want to climb one tree, the plum tree over there. I'd like to get some of that delicious fruit."

The baboon looked at the tree. He gave a low whistle. "I see what you mean." And off he dashed to the plum tree. Before the tortoise could turn around, Nyani was up the tree, busily picking plums and stuffing them into his mouth. Kamba crawled slowly toward him.

"Throw some down to me, please, Nyani," he called. But the baboon pretended not to hear. "Please let me have some," pleaded the tortoise.

"Oh, is that you down there, slow one? I have trouble hearing you at such a great distance." And the baboon continued to eat.

"You know I'm here. Throw me some plums,"

fumed Kamba. "Didn't I tell you about those plums.
I deserve a share."

Nyani climbed higher, eating as he went. He
knocked two plums off the tree and they fell near the
tortoise. Kamba ate them, then called in his loudest
voice, "You, up there. I know you can hear me. I
want more than two plums. There are more than
enough for you. Throw some to me."

But Nyani continued to eat. Finally, all the
plums were gone. The greedy baboon curled up in
a fork of the tree and went to sleep.

Kamba crept sadly home.

A few days later Nyani and Kamba met in the
forest. *"Jambo* to you, Nyani," called the tortoise.

"Good morning, slow one" replied the baboon.
"I hope you aren't angry with me."

"Not at all. I've been intending to ask you to
dinner. Won't you come to my house today? I found
some huge mushrooms."

"Mushrooms! My favorite food—next to plums.
Of course I'll come. Thank you so much."

"Come at sundown," called Kamba, and he
went on down the path.

When the tortoise arrived home, he set fire to

the grass around his house, so that a wide circle was blackened with soot. When the baboon arrived, Kamba greeted him. "Welcome to my feast, Nyani. I trust your hands are clean so that we may eat immediately."

Nyani looked at his hands which were covered with soot. "Perhaps I can wash somewhere."

"Certainly. Just go to the river there." The tortoise waved one front foot toward the stream. "Do hurry. I'm very hungry."

Nyani went across the burned strip to the water, washed carefully, and returned.

"Now let me see your hands," said Kamba. "Why they're dirty as ever!"

"So they are. But what am I to do with that burned strip to cross?"

"No one eats at my table with dirty hands. Try again."

Sadly the baboon returned to the river while Kamba called after him. "Do hurry, I'm getting terribly hungry."

While the baboon was washing a second time, the tortoise began to eat the mushrooms. Nyani returned with dirty hands. "Are you going to keep me washing at the river while you eat all the mush-rooms?" he asked.

"Didn't you keep me waiting at the foot of the tree while you ate all the plums?" asked Kamba.

Then Nyani knew he had received only what he deserved. He went home hungry.

True Tears

Long ago, when animals talked together, Nupe, the egret, and Woga, the raven, became friends. They searched for insects together and sailed through the sky in great swoops when the weather was fine.

Then came a day when Nupe met a handsome white egret and fell in love with him. The two flew away together to build a nest, leaving Woga alone.

Woga was lonely, so she began to look for a husband. It wasn't long until she met a shiny black raven, and they began building a stick nest.

I'm tired," sighed Woga after only a few hours of building. "This is too much work."

Her old friend, Nupe, flew by and heard her

muttering in the tree. "Hello there, Woga. Why so downcast? Aren't you making a nest?"

"Yes, I suppose so, but it's a very tiresome business."

"I think it's fun," laughed Nupe. "You should see us work. Our nest has a fine bottom already. Come and see it."

Woga took her husband and flew away to visit the new nest of her friend, Nupe.

"Jambo, Woga, how kind of you to come, especially at this busy time," said the egret.

"We grew tired of nest building—very tired," sighed Woga. "How I wish we were finished." With that she smoothed a stick into place on the side of the egret's half-finished home. "Yours looks lovely," she whispered just loudly enough for Nupe to hear. "Wish our nest were as fine as this."

"You should have built with us, Woga. You know, such good friends should be able to share a nest."

"Is it too late?" cried the raven. "We could help you finish now and could still use the same nest."

"Well, perhaps," said Nupe's husband. "Perhaps—"

So it was that the ravens helped the egrets build a nest. Nupe laid two eggs in it. Woga laid two, and the friends took turns sitting on the eggs and caring for the chicks when they hatched. At first the chicks were ugly, with pink featherless bodies, big heads, and huge beaks. All four parents kept busy finding food for them.

One day as Woga was bringing some choice insects to the nest, she noticed that the egret children were becoming quite handsome, growing pale feathers. Her raven babies had only stiff gray-black quills. As she watched the beautiful egret children, she became jealous. She said nothing to anyone about her feelings. But her husband noticed that she was less talkative than usual.

The chicks grew. When they were nearly ready to leave the nest, Woga waited for a time when Nupe and the two fathers were away. Then she told the two egret children that she would teach them to fly. Now they had gleaming white feathers and were more beautiful than ever.

Out of the nest scrambled the young egrets. They followed the raven on unsteady wings. But when they had made a few wobbly circles, they began to fly quite well.

Woga sailed high into the sky calling, "Come. Follow me, children." They followed. Woga flew to the home of the chief, with the two chicks close behind.

"What's this?" asked the chief from the door of his house, as the three birds flew close. "A black bird with white chicks? Seems a little odd."

"I salute you, oh, Chief," cried Woga, the raven. "I have brought my two beautiful children to pay their respects."

"They are handsome children indeed. But can they be yours?"

"Yes, of course. See how they follow me."

"Truly, they do follow you," said the chief. "Perhaps they are your children."

Nupe, the egret, returned to the nest and found her chicks missing. She inquired of her neighbors. They told her that Woga had flown away with her children. Nupe hurried to tell the chief, arriving just after the raven.

"Great Chief," called Nupe from the air. "I have come to report the theft of my chicks."

"Your chicks?" asked the chief.

"Yes. Have you seen Woga, the raven, with two white children?"

"Truly, they are in my house now. If these chicks do not belong to the raven why did they follow her?" inquired the chief.

"We have always been friends. We nested together. They know her well," said the egret. "Please, I beg of you, make her give them back."

The chief looked thoughtful. "I shall give you a test," he said. "Here is a clay pot. The chicks shall belong to the one of you who can fill the pot with tears."

Woga came out of the house and put her head over the pot. She wept loudly, wailing and flapping her wings. But she shed not one tear.

Then Nupe, the egret, put her head over the pot. She cried sorrowfully and filled it to the brim. Nupe shed many tears because her crying was real. Then she took her children and flew home with them.

When Woga, the raven, returned to the nest, her own children were gone. Her husband, when he found the chicks alone, had taken them away to live in another country and Woga never saw them again.

The Hunter's Bargain

Gatunga, the hunter, went out to see his traps. One trap was set near a patch of bush and in this bush lived Simba, the lion. For many days Simba watched as the hunter came by.

One day the hunter found an antelope in the trap. As Gatunga prepared to carry the meat home, the lion walked out of his hiding place.

"Jambo, great hunter," said Simba. "You have had luck today. That is a fine catch."

"Yes, indeed, Simba. My family is in need of meat."

Simba licked his lips greedily. "I, too, am hungry," he said.

"But aren't you the greatest hunter of all?"

"Yes, perhaps, but my luck has been bad," said the lion. "Give me some of the antelope."

"I would gladly give you some, but my children are hungry," said the man.

Simba growled. "Give me some of the meat or I shall eat you and the antelope, too."

"You who hunt so well shouldn't have to beg for meat," said Gatunga.

"I'm not begging. Give me the meat!" roared the lion.

"I'll make a bargain with you," said the hunter. "I'll give you the heart and the liver and any other inside parts of the antelope if you will let me go home with the rest of the meat."

"That's better," snarled Simba. "But I demand that you give me the insides of every animal you catch from now on. I shall be watching as you inspect your traps. Don't try to cheat me or I shall eat you and your catch!"

Frightened, Gatunga agreed. He removed the insides from the antelope, shouldered the remaining meat and went home.

Now it happened that Wanuki, the wife of the hunter, was very fond of liver and heart. When these choice bits were not inside the antelope her husband brought home, she was puzzled. She questioned Gatunga. "My husband, what have you done with the liver and heart?"

Gatunga didn't want to frighten Wanuki with the story of his bargain with Simba, the lion. He replied, "I must have lost them on the way home."

Each day Gatunga brought his catch home. Each day he came without the heart and the liver. Wanuki became more uneasy and suspicious. Finally, she determined to go and wait near one of the traps to see for herself who was getting a share of the meat. Just as the woman approached a large spring trap, she caught her foot in a root, stumbled and fell headlong into it. She struggled frantically, but the trap held her fast.

Out of the woods came Simba. "So!" he growled. "Today we have a new kind of game."

"What do you mean?" asked Wanuki.

"Don't you know that Gatunga gives me the inside parts of all he catches?"

"So you are the one who gets it?"

"Yes, and I'll have my share today," boasted Simba.

At that moment the hunter came in sight over the hill. He hurried to his trap. "Wanuki!" he shouted. "Why are you caught in the trap?"

"I came to find what was happening to the inside parts of all the game you caught."

"I'll release you," said Gatunga as he bent to untie the cords that held his wife.

"Wait!" hissed Simba. "Remember our bargain?"

"Surely, you wouldn't keep me to it now," gasped Gatunga.

"Part of all you catch," insisted the lion.

"Not this time. Not when the catch is my wife!"

"What's the dispute?" asked a small voice. Sungura, the hare, hopped out of the tall grass and stood before them.

As Sungura spoke, a strong wind ruffled the grass

and hissed through the trees.

"The lion demands my wife who is caught in the trap," said Gatunga, the hunter.

"It was a bargain," shouted Simba over the moaning of the wind.

"Eh?" asked Sungura. "I can't hear you."

"My wife is not game," insisted the hunter.

"Eh?" questioned the hare. "Come with me into yonder cave where we can talk away from the wind. Release the woman."

"A bargain must be kept," grumbled the lion as Gatunga cut the thongs holding Wanuki in the trap.

"Come on, Simba," shouted Sungura above the noise of the wind. "Surely you won't refuse to discuss this matter."

So Simba, Gatunga, and his wife went to the cave with Sungura. It was quiet there. Sungura listened while the lion and the hunter told of their strange agreement.

Sungura shook his head. "A bargain is a bargain. Yet you must admit, Simba, that you forced Gatunga into this one."

At that very moment the wind arose to a howling gale, swishing around the cave. "Help!" shouted Sungura. "The roof of the cave is falling in! We must hold it up. You, Simba, hold the roof with your head."

"I'm holding," said the frightened lion as he pushed with all his might on the top of the cave.

"Gatunga, you and Wanuki run to the woods for some sticks to prop the roof. Hurry!" shouted the hare with a wink. "Hurry!"

Gatunga, the hunter, and Wanuki, his wife, dashed away toward the village. The hare ran behind them. But Simba, the lion, held his head tightly against the roof of the cave. When the others did not return, he gave a snarl of rage and an angry leap, striking his head sharply against the cave entrance. With a howl of pain he sped off into the bush.

Since that time Simba, the lion, has made bargains with no one.

A Safe Home

One day long ago, Kando, the dove, met Njiwa, the hammerhead, in the bush. "*Jambo, Njiwa,*" said Kando. "How pleasant to see you here."

"Good morning, friend dove. I came to this hot dry place to hunt for insects."

"You should find plenty here, Njiwa. This bush is a very fine place to live," said the dove.

Njiwa, the hammerhead, was puzzled. "Why do you say that? It is very uncomfortable here. It's hot and dusty. I prefer to build my nest on the cool riverbank where my children won't gasp in the heat nor choke on the dust."

Kando chuckled, "Yes, I suppose you are comfortable by the river. But are you safe? What if the rains should come and the water should rise? What would happen to your family then?"

"There's never been such a rain since I can remember," said Njiwa. "Why should I expect it now?"

Kando shook his head sadly. "It could happen. My grandfather told of a time when rain fell for many days, flooding the river so that it overflowed the banks. Nests were destroyed. Birds and animals were carried away downstream."

"How dreadful," shuddered Njiwa.

"Why don't you move to safer ground?" asked the dove.

"Safer? But very uncomfortable. Thanks for the advice, friend. We'll stay where we are until rain threatens." The hammerhead looked at the sky. "See, not a cloud. It won't rain soon. And he flew away toward the river.

Not many days later, the hammerhead went into the bush again. He found so many insects that he went on and on, far from his home by the river.

Suddenly, there was a loud clap of thunder. A few huge raindrops made deep pits in the dusty soil. Njiwa remembered the advice of Kando. Frantically he flew toward home.

As the clouds gathered, Kando was catching insects for the family meal. He watched the sky. Then he said to his wife, "I'm worried about Njiwa and his family. Their nest is by the river. If the water should rise, they will all be destroyed."

"Perhaps you should go warn them."

"Yes, I'll go now." And Kando flew away toward the river just as the rain rushed down in great fast drops.

Now it happened that Njiwa and Kando arrived at the nest on the riverbank at the same instant. Rain was falling in sheets. Above the roar of the storm, Njiwa shouted, "So you've come to help me?"

"Hurry, let us move your family to safer ground back in the bush." The dove began to urge the young hammerheads from the nest.

Njiwa, his wife, and Kando flapped their wings and squawked in alarm. Just as the river water lapped at the nest, the chicks struggled to higher ground.

"How can I ever thank you, Kando?" asked Njiwa. "If I had only taken your advice in the first place."

"Thank me by being my friend, Njiwa. Come live near me in the bush. You may not be cool, but you will be safe."

So Njiwa, the hammerhead, built a new nest near Kando, the dove, in the dusty bush. They live there, friends to this day. In the cool evening, Kando and Njiwa can be heard telling their grandchildren about the great rain and how the dove helped save the family of the hammerhead.

The Jumper

One day Kamba, the tortoise, was on his way to the river when he met Tembo, the elephant. *"Jambo,* Tembo," said Kamba.

"Good morning, small one," said the elephant. "You are so far away down there that I can barely see you."

"And you are so very large and your eyes are so small, no wonder you can't see me," retorted Kamba.

"Oh, ho!" laughed Tembo. "It isn't because my eyes are small that I can't see you. It is only because you are nearly too small to see." He roared with laughter.

"Can you see the top of your own head?" asked the tortoise.

"Of course not. It is too far above my eyes."

"Yes, it is a very long way up, but small as I am, I can jump over your head."

Then Tembo, the elephant, laughed scornfully. "What a joke! Imagine you jumping over my head!"

"I can do it," insisted the tortoise.

"Try it," said Tembo.

"Not today. I've come a long way and I'm tired. Tomorrow, perhaps."

"Yes, yes, tomorrow. I can hardly wait to see the tiny tortoise jump over the huge elephant. What a joke that will be," roared Tembo.

"Maybe?" said Kamba. "I'll meet you here very early tomorrow morning."

"I'll be here. *Kwa heri.*"

Tembo returned his good-bye and rumbled off down the trail, shaking with laughter.

Next morning Kamba brought his wife, who looked exactly like him, and stationed her in the tall grass on one side of the trail.

Along came Tembo, his huge trunk swaying

from side to side and his small nearsighted eyes peering intently ahead of him.

"Are you there, Tortoise?" he called.

"Indeed, I am. I've been waiting for you," said Kamba. "See, I'm here beside the trail ready to jump."

"Should I stop here?" asked Tembo.

"Right there," agreed the tortoise. "Here I come." He gave a leap and shouted, "Ai-i-i-i," while on the other side of the trail his wife also gave a leap and shouted, "I-i-i!"

Kamba hid in the grass and Tembo saw only Kamba's wife.

"I don't see how you jumped so far," marveled Tembo. "You did it so quickly, too. Won't you do it again? Perhaps this time I can see you."

So Kamba's wife jumped first shouting, "Ai-i-i" and on the other side of the track Kamba jumped and cried, "I-i-i." Then the wife hid in the long grass.

"You are truly a jumper, Kamba," said the elephant. "Anyone who is so small and yet such a strong jumper deserves the respect of all the animals."

"Thank you, great one," said the tortoise.

From that day to this, Tembo, the elephant, has never teased Kamba, the tortoise, about being small. Tembo believes that the tortoise has strong magic which makes him a mighty jumper.

Spots

Many years ago before the animals were finished there were two lion cubs. One day, as they played beside the trail, they saw two painted warriors pass by. They were beautiful men, colored with the rust-red ochre of the clay banks.

"Oh, how handsome they are!" said Fisi, one of the lion brothers.

"What lovely colors they are wearing," said the other brother, Chui. "Wouldn't it be wonderful if we could be painted, too. We're just ugly light brown all over." In those far off days lion cubs had no spots.

I'd like to be painted, Fisi thought. Then he said to his brother, "Chui, I think I know how we can become as handsome as those warriors."

"You do? Tell me quickly," urged the brother. "I should like very much to be beautiful."

"Well, you know the river down at the end of the big trail where we go for a drink each evening."

"*Ndio.* But what of the river?"

"Be patient and I'll tell you," answered Fisi. "On the banks of the river, where the land breaks away sharply to the water, are red places in the earth. That red clay is the beautiful color that those warriors were wearing. Let's get some of that red earth, mix it with water, and paint each other."

"*Ndio,*" agreed Chui. "Let us go now."

The two lion cubs started toward the river. They stopped at the warrior's *shamba* on the way and took a large gourd.

"He won't miss just one," said Fisi. "This will make a fine paint pot."

Chui and Fisi took the seeds out of the gourd, then filled it with the red earth of the riverbank. They mixed in just enough water to make a nice thick paint. Then they picked a stiff grass head for a paint brush.

"Now we're ready to begin. I'll paint you first," said Fisi.

Chui agreed. He stood very still while Fisi carefully brushed the red ochre in round even circles of spots. When he finished, Fisi admired his handiwork. "You are indeed handsome. Never was a lion so beautiful. Go to the riverbank and look at your reflection in the water."

Chui trotted to the bank and gazed at himself for a long time. Never had he seen such a gorgeous creature.

"Come on, Chui. Paint me," called Fisi.

Chui trotted back, took up the grass brush and began painting spots on Fisi's head. When he had finished the head and was starting the neck, they heard a terrified shout.

"Run, run! Run for your lives!" And Sungura, the hare, came scurrying by, running from that enemy of all the bush people, a grass fire.

Terrified, Chui flung the paint pot at his brother and both of them ran for their lives.

When they were finally out of danger, they sat down to rest. "Oh, Fisi, I'm so sorry! I've ruined your spots. They are uneven and messy, not beautiful like mine," gasped Chui.

"Never mind," said his brother. "At least they are spots and we are safe from the fire."

After the brothers had rested, they made their way back home to find their family. But, alas, mother and father lion didn't know them and wouldn't believe that these spotted creatures were their children. The parents sent the young cubs away into the bush.

Chui, the beautiful brother, became the father of all the leopards.

Fisi, with his uneven spots, became the hyena, and all his children and grandchildren have the same spots.

King of the Mice

Once long ago the mice gathered to choose a king. Each mouse village suggested the name of its favorite elder. The shrew mice proposed their wisest old man, a mouse with a handsome long nose. The vole mice proposed Mbeva, who was wise. They voted. When all the votes were counted, Mbeva, the vole mouse, and Umulumba, the shrew mouse, had each received the same number.

Then Umulumba, the shrew mouse, said in a loud voice, "I must be king of all the mice, for only I can rule justly."

"*Hapana, hapana,*" shouted the vole mice. "We don't want that long nose poking into all our affairs. Let us vote again."

"We should gather for a great feast next dry time," suggested Panya, the house mouse. "We can vote again. Some of us may change our minds."

"*Ndio, ndio, ndio,*" shouted many voices.

So when another rain had passed, the mice met again to choose between the vole mouse and the shrew mouse. Every mouse brought food—nuts, grass seeds, maize, and beans and placed it in a huge pile. They held a great *barazza.* After they had eaten for a very long time, they began to argue. All the mice squeaked and shouted, each trying to win votes for his favorite.

While the other mice were eating and disputing, Mbeva, the vole mouse, quietly carried food away from the pile and buried it behind a little hill. Soon all the food was gone.

"What shall we do now?" asked Panya. "The food is gone, and we still haven't chosen a king. We can't stay here much longer without something to eat."

"Perhaps someone knows where there is a good

store of maize nearby," suggested Mbeva. "How about you, Umulumba? You want to be our king. If you are so wise, show us where to find food."

"I brought what I had," replied the shrew mouse. "If you are too greedy to make it last, then you must all go hungry."

Quietly, Mbeva moved around to the center of the group. "Would you really like more food?" he asked.

"*Ndio, ndio, ndio,*" shouted all the mice.

"Then dig behind that little hill," said Mbeva.

The mice scurried around the hill and dug. They found the food that the vole mouse had hidden. When they had eaten it, they were still hungry.

"More! Show us more," they squeaked.

But Mbeva shook his head. "That would not be wise. I'm saving the rest for a time of famine. My people will always be safe from hunger if some food is left buried."

"He is wise," said Panya, the house mouse. "Let him be our king."

"Yes, yes," shouted all the mice. "The vole shall be king of the mice."

Mbeva, the vole mouse, ruled for many years,

but he never revealed the hiding place of his food stores. When questioned he always said, "I'm saving food for a time of greater hunger."

But that time never came. Ever since, the other mice search the fields day after day hunting for the food that the vole mouse is saving.

The Deceitful Leopard

Long ago, Chui, the leopard, and his small cousin, Jila, the genet cat, were friends. Chui visited Jila often, showing him how to chase his tail and how to hunt. Flattered by the attentions of his handsome big cousin, Jila failed to notice that sometimes Chui was greedy and not quite honest.

One day, as the leopard and the genet romped together at the edge of a small clearing in the bush, Chui said, "Let's take a journey, Jila. Let us walk toward the setting sun."

"Wonderful!" shouted the genet. "What an adventure that will be! And in such good company, too."

Chui strutted. "Good company I always aim to be," he boasted.

Jila cavorted impatiently around his big cousin. "When can we start? Let's go."

"If you don't stand still, you will be so tired that you won't be able to make the journey," scolded Chui.

"Well?" demanded Jila. "When will it be?"

Chui laughed until his handsome spotted sides rippled in the sunshine. "Right now, my impatient cousin. Immediately!"

So the two set out. They crossed streams, woodlands, and plains. When the last rays of the sun were sinking beyond the rim of the earth, Jila, the genet, said to Chui, the leopard, "I'm tired. Let's find a place to sleep."

"I'm more hungry than tired," said the leopard. "Let us first find something to eat."

"You're always hungry, Chui. Don't you know you can't hunt tonight? Wait until morning and I will hunt with you."

"I'll be hungrier than ever by morning," grumbled Chui.

"You're big and strong. You can wait," said the little genet.

"Big and strong I am," boasted Chui. "I guess I'll have to wait. Now let's find a place to sleep."

The two cats moved on through the dusk for a few paces. There in front of them they saw a clearing. "Man!" they exclaimed together. "Perhaps we can sleep near one of the houses. It would provide shelter from the night wind," suggested Jila.

"A splendid idea," said the leopard.

"Look, Chui. There is a sheep pen. We can sleep beside that. No one will see us or bother us if we sleep on the side away from the house."

"You are right, Cousin."

"I shall be glad to sleep. I am very tired." The genet yawned wearily.

"I'm still hungry," said the leopard.

"Forget about food until morning, then we can both hunt."

Chui and Jila settled down to sleep beside the sheep pen. Inside they could hear the sheep moving, sometimes baaing softly. Jila was soon sound asleep.

Chui moved about restlessly. He was too hungry to sleep. The bleating of the sheep and the pains in his stomach kept him awake.

At last the leopard arose and crept softly to a low place in the thorn fence of the sheep pen. He bounded in on his soft cat paws, seized a sheep, and was out before the animal knew he had come.

After Chui had eaten his fill, he muttered "Now what shall I do? They are sure to miss that sheep in the morning. They know leopards like sheep. I must run away."

He started into the bush. But he was tired, too tired to go on. Slowly Chui returned to the dead sheep. He took some of the blood and smeared it on the mouth of Jila, and lay down beside his sleeping cousin.

That morning, very early, the man came to take his sheep out to graze. As the animals came through the gate, he counted them, as he always did. There were only twenty! Yesterday there had been twenty-one.

"Wife," he shouted, "Children! Come quickly

and help me find the thief. Someone has stolen one of our sheep."

Out of the house tumbled the sleepy family. "Who has stolen a sheep? How do you know? When?" they shouted all at once.

"Don't ask so many questions. Just help me find the thief. One sheep is missing." Around the pen they went, looking for tracks.

Suddenly the smallest boy stopped. "A-i-i-i-i! There he is!"

Against the thorn fence, still sound asleep, was Jila. The blood stains showed red on his mouth. A few feet beyond him Chui slept soundly.

"Thief!" shouted the man and ran toward Jila with his sharp spear. Just in time the little genet aroused.

"What is it?" he asked sleepily.

"You know what it is," said the man. "You have eaten one of my sheep."

"I have eaten nothing since day before yesterday."

"You have given yourself away by the blood on your mouth," said the man.

"There can be no blood on my mouth. I have

eaten nothing," insisted the genet. "My cousin, Chui, who sleeps beside me, will swear to this."

Chui awoke and rubbed his eyes. "What will I swear, Jila?" he asked. "How can I swear to anything when I have been asleep all night?"

"Please, Chui, tell them I didn't eat their sheep," pleaded Jila.

Chui looked sharply at the genet. "You ask me to say you didn't eat their sheep. Why your very face gives you away. It is smeared with fresh blood."

With a howl of despair and rage, the little genet dashed into the bush, running toward home as fast as he could go.

Chui, the leopard, also went home, but more slowly because he had eaten so much meat.

Several days later Jila was out in the bush hunting. As he trotted through the tall grass he thought to himself. How did I get that blood on my face? I wasn't hungry. I didn't kill a sheep. Chui must have deceived me. Now I must avoid him and hunt alone. Next time his tricks may prove my undoing.

So it is to this day. The cousins avoid each other. The genet hunts by day and the leopard hunts by night.

The Giraffe's Neck

Long ago when things were just beginning and the animals were not quite finished, Twiga, the giraffe, had a short neck, not much longer than the neck of Kongoni, the hartebeeste.

The giraffe and the hartebeeste spent much time together out on the plains eating grass. Kongoni loved grass, but Twiga often tired of such fare and hunted for small trees, reaching high into the branches to eat the fresh green leaves.

One day Twiga and Kongoni were grazing near a stream. Kongoni, as usual, was eating grass.

Twiga found an especially tender thorn tree and was stuffing himself on the leaves and prickly thorns. Higher and higher he reached, until his front feet were off the ground, and he teetered dangerously on the tips of his back hooves.

"What you need is a longer neck," laughed Kongoni.

"Or some shorter trees," agreed the giraffe. And he pushed his head into the tree so far that only his hind feet and tail could be seen.

"If that giraffe knew what was good, he wouldn't eat leaves," muttered the hartebeeste. "Anyone knows grass is the best food there is."

From inside the bushy tree came a constant munch-crunch as Twiga chewed leaves. "If that Kongoni knew what was good he wouldn't always eat grass," he said to himself. "I'll take a delicious meal of leaves any day." And he stretched higher.

Now, along came Swara, the bushbuck. *"Jambo* friend Kongoni," he said. "Who is that curious creature hiding in the tree? The legs and tail look like Twiga, but I can't see the rest of him. What is he doing?"

Kongoni laughed. "That is Twiga. He is eating leaves."

"Eating leaves! How curious. I prefer grass. It is easier to chew, tastes better, and is much easier to reach."

"I think Twiga has queer tastes," declared the bushbuck, as he nibbled the green shoots at his feet.

Kongoni, the hartebeeste, finished his lunch and looked around. It suddenly became dark. He looked at the sky and saw a black cloud rolling toward them. He watched it come, then called out, "Quick, Twiga, run! A wind storm is coming. Run, Swara!"

Swara, the bushbuck, ran quickly out of the path of the funnel shaped cloud. Kongoni, the hartebeeste, called again to the giraffe. "Run, Twiga! Run for your life. A tornado is coming." But the giraffe couldn't hear him. His head was too deeply buried in the branches of the tree.

Whoosh, came the wind. Whirling around and around ever faster and faster. It came to the tree where the giraffe was eating, caught it up, roots and all, and pulled it into the air. Twiga struggled, but couldn't free his head from the branches. Around he whirled with his head fast in the tree and the rest of him dangling below.

"Help, help, help!" gasped Twiga. But his words were lost in the howl of the wind. At last, when the tornado had passed, down came the tree to the earth. It hit the ground, struggling giraffe and all, with a rousing thump. Giving a great kick and a jerk, Twiga freed himself from his trap and gasped, "How frightening! I'm stretched all over. My legs wobble!" Then he looked down, "Ai-iii-i-i-i," he screeched. "How far it is to the ground!" Then he rubbed his neck. "My neck! What has happened to my neck?"

Kongoni and Swara, who had watched the giraffe's journey from the safety of the plain, ran to the spot where he fell.

"What happened to you?" asked Kongoni in amazement. "I do believe your neck has stretched."

"Yes, I fear it has," groaned Twiga.

"Fear? Why it's a blessing," declared Swara. "Now you'll have no trouble at all eating the leaves from the tallest trees."

"How wonderful," laughed the giraffe, as he rubbed his new long neck against a tree trunk. "You are very right, my friend. It is a blessing. The newest green leaves won't be too high for me to reach."

So Twiga, the giraffe, continued to eat the leaves from the trees. In fact, he quit eating grass altogether.

Gathering Salt

Once long ago, when men and animals talked together, there lived a great and powerful chief whose name was Kambura. Kambura had many children. Loveliest of them all was his beautiful daughter, Wanami, whose skin was a velvety blackness, whose eyes shone like the midnight stars, and whose teeth were as white as the egret's wing. Wanami had many suitors. Some of them came as animals. In those far off days, it was an easy matter for men to change themselves into animals.

Kambura, the chief, wanted a husband who was

both cunning and swift. Nothing less would do for his daughter. Most favored among the suitors were Kamba, the tortoise, and Kipalala, the fish eagle.

One day both Kamba and Kipalala appeared at the house of the chief. Kamba spoke first, "Oh, mighty Kambura, can you not see that I would make a good and steady husband for your lovely daughter?"

But Kipalala spread his wide wings, preened his shining feathers, and said, "He is dull beside me. He is slow as well. Wanami would grow tired of him."

"Enough of your boasting," said the chief. "We shall see who is better. Wanami shall become the wife of the first one of you who can go to the seashore and bring back a packet of sea salt."

"Ho, ho," laughed Kipalala, the fish eagle. "Imagine what will happen now! I can go ten times before that pokey tortoise makes one trip."

"Please, Kambura, give me some time to practice. Perhaps I can learn to run as fast as the fish eagle flies," begged Kamba. "I think I might be ready after two rains."

"Agreed," said the chief. "After two rains, you are both to appear before me to begin the journey to the sea. The one who wins the race shall have my daughter."

"I'll win," bragged Kipalala. "A tortoise can never run as fast as the fish eagle flies."

Kamba began to make his plans. He immediately set out for the seashore. Every few miles he stopped at the house of a relative, and with each he left a message. When he arrived at the shore, he gathered a packet of salt, then went to spend the night at the house of a cousin who lived nearby. While visiting he told his story. He arranged to have the cousin out gathering salt on the shore on the day appointed for the contest. Then Kamba, the tortoise, made his way slowly home, carrying his pack of salt with him.

After two rains, Kipalala and Kamba went to the house of Kambura, the chief, to begin the journey. They set out at the same time. The eagle soared into the sky and was soon only a speck in the distance. Kamba walked slowly in the same direction.

After Kipalala had flown a short time, he muttered to himself, "Wonder where that slow tortoise is now? I've plenty of time for a look." He swooped down, peered at the ground and called out, "Kamba, are you there?" The cousin of Kamba who lived nearby called back, "Yes, I am here."

Kipalala was puzzled. How could that pokey

tortoise have come so far? He hurried on, but was too curious to keep flying. Three more times he came near the earth calling loudly, "Kamba, are you there?" And each time he received the same reply, "Indeed, yes! Here I am."

At last the blue waters of the sea appeared. Kipalala hurried. When he started down to get his salt from the shore, there below him was a tortoise quietly gathering salt. Snatching his salt, the fish eagle soared into the sky and flew home as fast as his wings could take him.

Kamba, the tortoise, watched from the bushes. Late in the afternoon he saw Kipalala coming, a dark speck in the sky. Taking his packet of salt from its hiding place, he hurried to the house of Kambura, the chief. He called loudly, "I have come, great chief. Here is the salt."

At that moment, the chief and his daughter saw the fish eagle coming.

"How can it be that you, a tortoise, arrived before Kipalala?" asked Kambura.

"I have learned to run fast, oh, chief," said Kamba.

When Kipalala saw that the tortoise had beaten him, he was very angry. "You, Kamba, must have

won by trickery, but I don't know how. Beware of my anger!" The disappointed fish eagle flew away into the sky.

"You promised Wanami to the winner, great chief," said Kamba, the tortoise. "I claim her for my wife."

"But you will make a poor husband. Your life will always be in danger, for Kipalala is angry and will make trouble for you," said the chief.

"He won't be able to find us, for we shall live where he cannot get us," declared Kamba. Then he took the beautiful Wanami by the hand, and together they dived into the river which ran by the house of the chief.

As Kambura watched them sink below the waters, his daughter changed into a tortoise like Kamba. There they live to this day, safe from the anger of Kipalala, the fish eagle.

The Monkey's Heart

There was once a monkey called Kima who lived beside the sea in a great mbuyu tree. The branches of this tree were so wide that they hung far out over the water. On the tree grew delicious fruit of which Kima was very fond.

Beneath the spreading branches of the mbuyu tree, in the warm blue water near the shore, lived Papa, the shark. Day after day he watched the monkey eating the fruit. Then one day Papa called to the monkey, "Please won't you throw some down to me?"

"Who is it?" asked Kima.

"I am Papa, the shark. I come every day to lie in the warm water near the shore. I'd like to taste that fruit. It looks delicious."

"It is. Here, catch this one," and Kima dropped a large fruit to the shark.

"*Asante*," said Papa. "It tastes delicious."

So that is how Kima, the monkey, and Papa, the shark, became friends. Each day the shark came to the warm shore beneath the mbuyu tree. Kima dropped fruit to him and they ate and talked together. Each evening Papa returned to his home in the deep water of the sea.

One day when the shark appeared beneath the tree, he called to the monkey, "Kima, my friend, won't you come to my house to dine today?"

"I'd like to come, Papa, but can't go into the water. I don't know how to swim and would surely drown."

"I know you can't swim," said the shark. "Don't worry about that. You may ride on my back."

The monkey came down from the tree. The shark swam very close to shore. Kima climbed upon his back and they started out to sea. When they had

gone only a short distance, Papa said, "I have something to tell you, something I hate to say."

"What is it?" asked Kima.

"I have tricked you. It is all my fault because
I told my people of our friendship."

"What do you mean, Papa?"

"I was sent to get you, Kima. Our chief is very
ill. The great medicine man said that only a monkey's heart will cure him."

"What?" gasped Kima.

"They made me come," insisted Papa. "I do not
wish you harm."

"You've made a mistake, my friend," said Kima.
"Haven't you heard that a monkey never takes his
heart with him when he travels from home? Mine is
back in the mbuyu tree where I live."

"In that case, we must go back to get it," said
the shark.

"We must go back," agreed Kima. "It would
never do for you to return home without it."

The huge fish turned around and carried the
monkey back to his tree on the shore. Kima caught
hold of a low-hanging branch and swung himself into
the tree. He disappeared among the thick branches.

After a long silence, Papa called, "Haven't you found your heart?"

There was no answer.

The shark waited, then called again, "Why does it take you so long, Kima?"

Still there was only silence.

At last Papa called in a very loud voice, "Kima are you there? Have you no ears?"

Then from the green branches of the mbuyu tree came the monkey's answer. "For those who would betray my friendship I have neither heart nor ears."